The Magic School Bus

Explores the Senses

S
E E
HEAR
SMELL TASTE
TOUCH

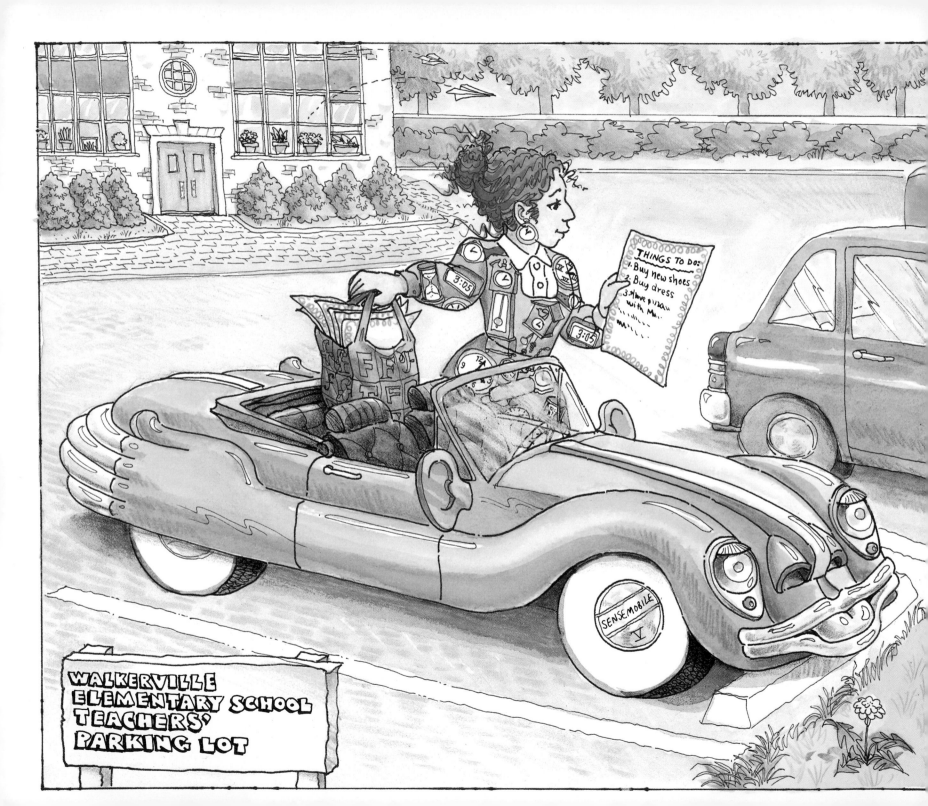

The Magic School Bus

Explores the Senses

By Joanna Cole
Illustrated by Bruce Degen

Scholastic Inc.
New York · Toronto · London · Auckland · Sydney · Mexico City · New Delhi · Hong Kong

For his careful reading of the manuscript and illustrations, we thank Bruce Rideout, Ph.D.,
Professor of Behavioral Neuroscience, Ursinus College. His untiring attention to the details
helped us enormously. Thanks also to David A. Stevens, Ph.D.; Matthew D. Paul, M.D.;
Brian J. Silverlieb, V.M.D.; Lorraine Hopping Egan; Karen Pierce;
and, as always, Stephanie Calmenson.

ISBN 0-590-44698-3

Published by Scholastic Inc.
SCHOLASTIC, THE MAGIC SCHOOL BUS, and associated logos
are trademarks and/or registered trademarks of Scholastic Inc.

12 11 10 9   1 2 3 4/0

Printed in the U.S.A.   08
First Scholastic paperback printing, September 1999

The text type was set in 15 point Bookman Light.
The illustrator used pen and ink, watercolor,
color pencil, and gouache for the paintings in this book.

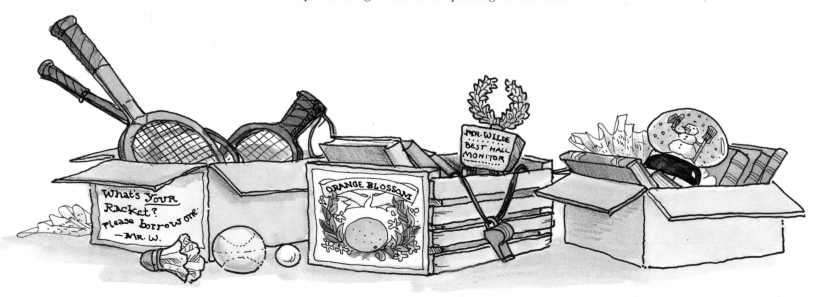

For David Hashmall, whose friendly wisdom
and guidance always make perfect *sense!*
— J.C. & B.D.

WITHOUT OUR SENSES, WE'D BE OUT OF IT
by Carlos

If someone could not see, hear, feel, taste, or smell, that person would not be able to tell anything about the outside world.

Our class was studying the senses — how people and animals know what's going on around them. We were doing experiments and writing reports. We were even learning a song about the senses to sing at an important parent-teacher meeting. The day before the meeting, we practiced our song twenty times.

HEAR A SCHOOL BELL RING, SEE A BRIGHT LIGHT SHINE, TOUCH A CAT'S SOFT FUR, YOU'LL BE JUST IN TIME...

TO COME TO YOUR SENSES!

SEE

TASTE

TOUCH

SMELL

HEAR

It would have been easier if we had an ordinary teacher.
But we don't — we have Ms. Frizzle.
Looking at her dress made us forget the tune.
Her shoes made us forget the words.
And her wacky personality made us forget
almost everything else!

CLASS, THE SHOW IS TOMORROW EVENING.

TASTE A SCHOOL BELL RING...

SMELL A BRIGHT LIGHT SHINE...

SOMEHOW, I DON'T THINK WE'LL BE READY....

My favorite smell by Phoebe

EVERY ANIMAL NEEDS SENSES
by Arnold
Without senses, an animal could not find food or escape from danger.

I SEE YOU! I HEAR YOU! I SMELL YOU!

I SEE, HEAR, AND SMELL YOU, TOO!

EVEN THE TINIEST ANIMALS HAVE SENSES
by Keesha
One-celled animals have simple senses. They can tell when their surroundings are too hot, too cold, or too poisonous.
Then they turn around and go the other way!

I MAY BE MICROSCOPIC, BUT I'M SENSITIVE!

7

WHICH SENSES ARE MOST IMPORTANT?
by Phil

Different kinds of animals rely on different senses.

Seeing is most important to birds. They can't find food if they can't see it!

Bats use hearing to tell them where they're going. They can't hunt if their ears are blocked.

Snakes smell the air with their forked tongues. If a snake's tongue isn't working, it's hard for it to find its prey.

THAT SMELLS YUMMY!

8

When the school day was over, we went outside to warm up for a game. After a while, Ms. Frizzle came out and got in her car. At the same moment, Mr. Wilde, our new assistant principal, called to us, "See you at the meeting tonight." "Tonight!?" we groaned. "Ms. Frizzle thinks it's tomorrow!" "I have to tell her," said Mr. Wilde. But it was too late. The Friz was already driving away.

MR. WILDE IS A GREAT ASSISTANT PRINCIPAL, BUT I DON'T THINK HE CAN HANDLE THE BUS....

HE DOES SEEM LIKE A QUIET SORT OF GUY.

HE NEEDS OUR HELP!

LET'S GO!

"I've got to catch up with Ms. Frizzle!" said Mr. Wilde.
To our surprise, he got behind the wheel of our bus.
Believe us, we've had a lot of experience with that bus.
We couldn't let Mr. Wilde drive it. Not all by himself!
After all, he's only an assistant principal —
he's not Ms. Frizzle!
We all jumped on board.

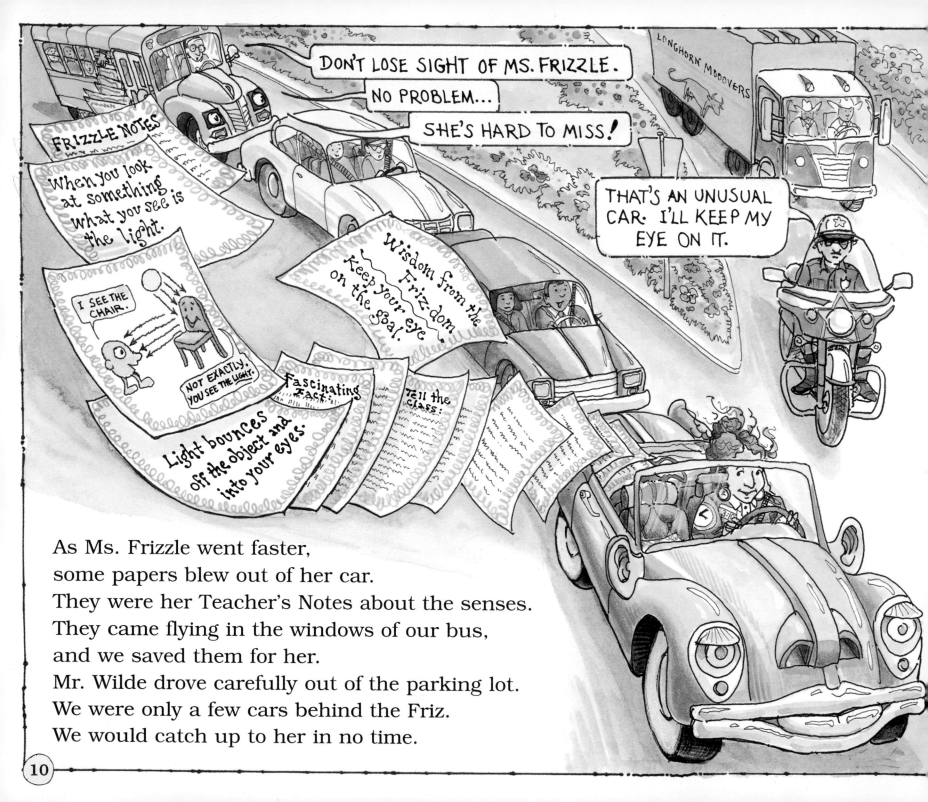

As Ms. Frizzle went faster,
some papers blew out of her car.
They were her Teacher's Notes about the senses.
They came flying in the windows of our bus,
and we saved them for her.
Mr. Wilde drove carefully out of the parking lot.
We were only a few cars behind the Friz.
We would catch up to her in no time.

Then Mr. Wilde saw a little green switch on the dashboard.
"Green means go," he muttered to himself,
reaching for the switch.
"DON'T TOUCH IT!" we warned.
But it was too late. Mr. Wilde flipped the switch.
He had never been in a school bus like this one before.
But we had — plenty of times.
We knew that something impossible was going to happen.
And it did. The bus began to shrink.

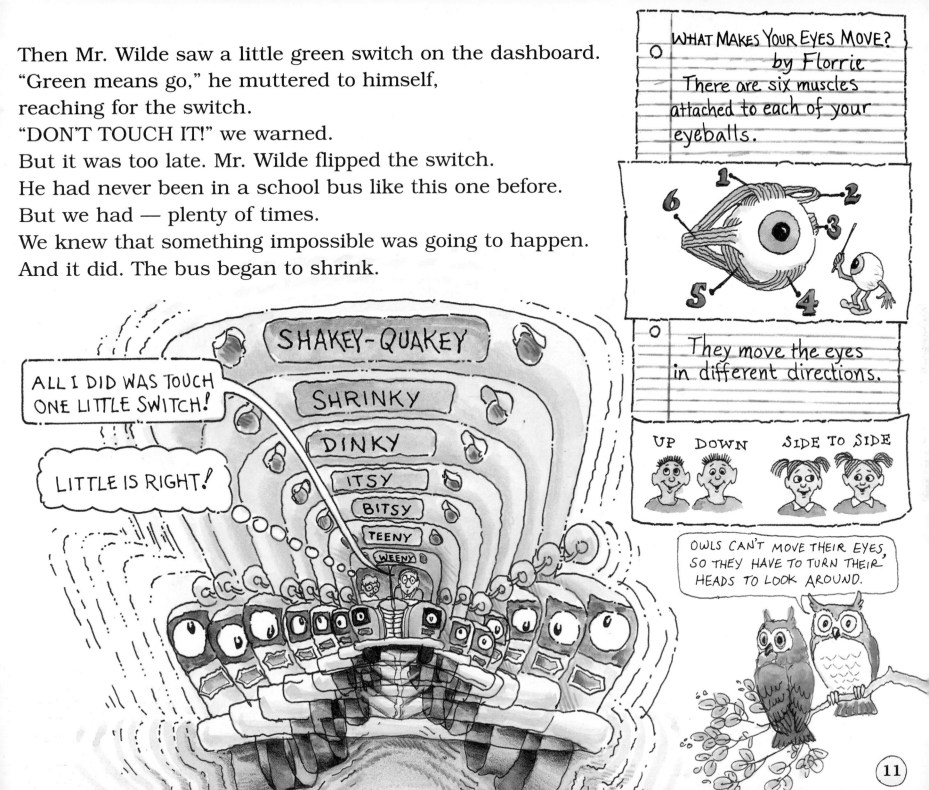

ALL I DID WAS TOUCH ONE LITTLE SWITCH!

LITTLE IS RIGHT!

SHAKEY-QUAKEY

SHRINKY

DINKY

ITSY

BITSY

TEENY

WEENY

WHAT MAKES YOUR EYES MOVE?
by Florrie
There are six muscles attached to each of your eyeballs.

They move the eyes in different directions.

UP   DOWN

SIDE TO SIDE

OWLS CAN'T MOVE THEIR EYES, SO THEY HAVE TO TURN THEIR HEADS TO LOOK AROUND.

11

YOUR IRIS IS ALL MUSCLE...
by Gregory
The colored part of your eye-- the iris-- is a ring of muscle.

...BUT YOUR PUPIL IS NOTHING AT ALL!
The dark spot in the middle of your iris is actually an opening into your eye-- the pupil. Your pupil is protected by a tough, clear layer called the cornea.

IRIS

PUPIL

The bus shrank until it was no bigger
than a speck of dust.
A stiff breeze started up and blew us into the air.
Ahead, we saw a big blue circle.
In the middle of the circle was a black dot.
It was a giant eye!
The eye belonged to a police officer,
and we blew right into it!

OOPS! I HAVE SOMETHING IN MY EYE.

Before the officer could blink us out,
Mr. Wilde saw a rainbow-colored lever.
"LEAVE THE LEVER ALONE!" we yelled.
But he couldn't resist. He pulled the lever,
and the bus slid smoothly through the cornea —
the clear covering that protects the iris and the pupil.
Beyond the cornea, we passed through a sea of
clear liquid ... past the blue iris ... and through the pupil.
"Who knew driving a bus was so much fun?"
asked Mr. Wilde.

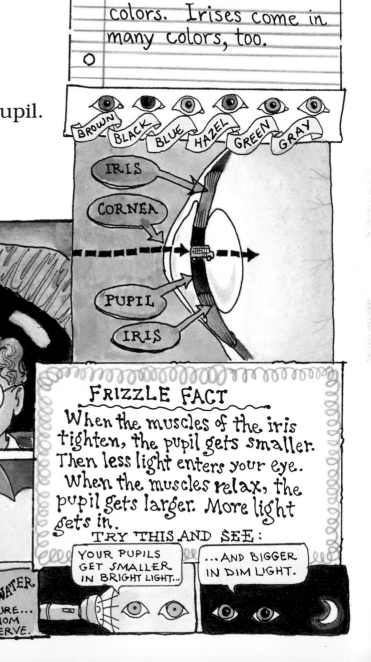

A WORD FROM DOROTHY ANN
Iris comes from a word that means "rainbow". A rainbow has lots of colors. Irises come in many colors, too.

BROWN BLACK BLUE HAZEL GREEN GRAY

IRIS
CORNEA
PUPIL
IRIS

FRIZZLE FACT
When the muscles of the iris tighten, the pupil gets smaller. Then less light enters your eye. When the muscles relax, the pupil gets larger. More light gets in.
TRY THIS AND SEE:
YOUR PUPILS GET SMALLER IN BRIGHT LIGHT...
...AND BIGGER IN DIM LIGHT.

I'M DRIVING INTO AN EYE?? I CAN'T BELIEVE IT, PHOEBE!

AT MY OLD SCHOOL PUPILS NEVER WENT INTO A PUPIL!

MY CLASS IS REALLY INTO THE HUMAN EYE.

THEY'D BETTER LOOK OUT!

MOM'S

MOM'S SPRING WATER COLD AND PURE... JUST LIKE MOM USED TO SERVE.

YOUR EYE IS LIKE A LIVING CAMERA
by Phil

Your pupil is like the camera's aperture (opening), which lets in light.

Your lens is like the camera's glass lens, which focuses the light.

Your retina is like the film, which changes when light hits it.

Mr. Wilde was going wild!
"I should have been a school bus driver
instead of an assistant principal!" he exclaimed,
as we slipped through the clear lens of the eye.
We weren't the only ones going through.
Rays of light went through, also.
The lens focused the light to make a sharp picture
on the retina — a layer of cells on the back of the eye.

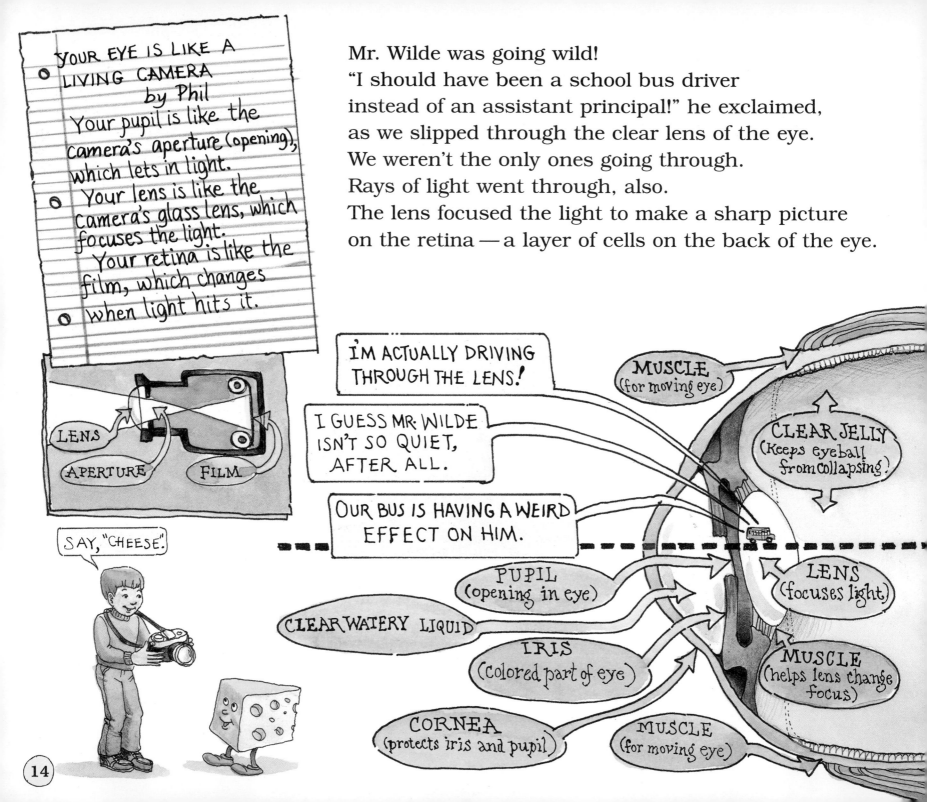

LENS

APERTURE

FILM

SAY, "CHEESE!"

I'M ACTUALLY DRIVING THROUGH THE LENS!

I GUESS MR. WILDE ISN'T SO QUIET, AFTER ALL.

OUR BUS IS HAVING A WEIRD EFFECT ON HIM.

MUSCLE (for moving eye)

CLEAR JELLY (keeps eyeball from collapsing)

PUPIL (opening in eye)

CLEAR WATERY LIQUID

IRIS (colored part of eye)

LENS (focuses light)

MUSCLE (helps lens change focus)

CORNEA (protects iris and pupil)

MUSCLE (for moving eye)

"Let's go to the retina," said Mr. Wilde,
gunning the engine.
There was no stopping him now!
The Teacher's Notes said the retina is made up of
special cells called rods and cones.
These cells change the light that falls on them.
The pattern of light becomes a pattern
of nerve signals going to the brain.
"It's like translating one language into another," said Tim.
"The rods and cones translate
'light language' into 'nerve language.'"

RODS AND CONES:
WHAT'S THE DIFFERENCE?
by Ralphie
We need both rods and cones for good vision.
Cone cells let us see clearly and in color. They work best in bright light.
When we use **rod cells** our vision is blurry and we cannot see colors.
However, we need rods to see in dim light.

RETINA
(where image forms)

WE'RE USING OUR OWN CONES AND RODS TO SEE SOMEONE ELSE'S CONES AND RODS.

CONES ARE GOOD FOR DAY VISION.

RODS ARE GOOD AT NIGHT.

SCHOOL BUS
(Not usually in eye)

PROTECTING LAYERS

ACTUAL SIZE:
The retina in your eye is no thicker than a page in this book!

OPTIC NERVE

ROD

CONE

Mr. Wilde had forgotten all about delivering his message to the Friz. All he cared about was driving the bus. All we cared about was finding Ms. Frizzle. Keesha flipped through the Teacher's Notes, trying to figure out where we were.

"Look! Here's a map of the retina," she said. "'The spot in the center of the retina is the fovea. That's the part of the eye we use when we look directly at something.'"

WHY YOUR FOVEAS LOOK SHARP
            by Shirley
The fovea is covered with cone cells--only cone cells. They are good for seeing sharply.

FOVEAS IN ACTION
Try this:
Watch people reading. Do their eyes move back and forth? Why?
People's eyes move to keep their foveas aimed at the words they are reading.

"What's the other round spot on the retina?" we asked.
"It's called the blind spot," answered Keesha.
Everyone is blind in that little spot of the eye.
It's where all the nerves in the eye come together.
They form a bundle called the optic nerve,
which runs from the eye to the brain."
A smile spread over Mr. Wilde's face
as he steered the bus into the optic nerve.

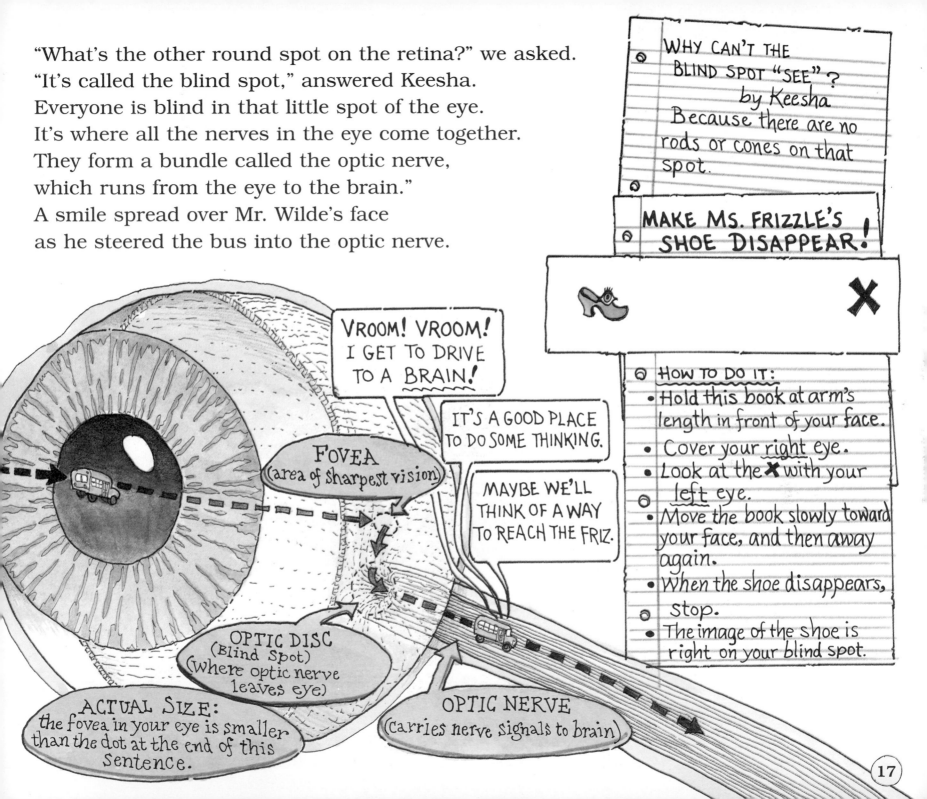

VROOM! VROOM!
I GET TO DRIVE
TO A BRAIN!

IT'S A GOOD PLACE
TO DO SOME THINKING.

MAYBE WE'LL
THINK OF A WAY
TO REACH THE FRIZ.

FOVEA
(area of sharpest vision)

OPTIC DISC
(Blind Spot)
(where optic nerve
leaves eye)

ACTUAL SIZE:
the fovea in your eye is smaller
than the dot at the end of this
sentence.

OPTIC NERVE
(carries nerve signals to brain)

WHY CAN'T THE
BLIND SPOT "SEE"?
by Keesha
Because there are no
rods or cones on that
spot.

MAKE MS. FRIZZLE'S
SHOE DISAPPEAR!

✗

HOW TO DO IT:
• Hold this book at arm's
length in front of your face.
• Cover your right eye.
• Look at the ✗ with your
left eye.
• Move the book slowly toward
your face, and then away
again.
• When the shoe disappears,
stop.
• The image of the shoe is
right on your blind spot.

17

YOUR BRAIN -- IT'S NOT
JUST FOR THINKING
by Phoebe
A thin wrinkled layer
covers your brain like
the rind of a melon.
This is the cerebral cortex.

CORTEX

Brain cut
in half

Different parts of the
cortex let you think, talk,
remember, move, see,
hear, taste, smell, and
touch.

ACTUAL SIZE
The cortex is no thicker
than the cover of a hardcover
book. If it were spread out
flat, it would be the size
of a small tablecloth.

We rolled out onto the surface of the brain —
it's called the cerebral cortex.
"We have to keep track of the Friz," said Ralphie.
"Look for the part of the cortex
that gets messages from the eyes."
Everyone scrambled off the bus and spread out.
Wanda called from the back of the brain, "Here it is!"
We ran to join Wanda on the vision center of the brain.
Somehow we saw what Officer Jones saw!

WE FOUND
THE BRAIN'S
VISION CENTER.

NOW WE CAN SEE
MS. FRIZZLE!

SO THAT'S WHERE SHE
GETS HER CLOTHES...

LIGHT

OPTIC
NERVE

WHERE IS YOUR VISION CENTER?
Put your hand on the back
of your head just above
your neck. Your hand will be
right over the vision center.

FRIZZLE FACT
You can't see with
your eyes alone.
You need your
brain, too!

There was Ms. Frizzle in a dress shop,
buying a dress with optical illusions on it.
We called for help, but of course she couldn't hear us.
She didn't know that Mr. Wilde was driving the bus.
She didn't know that her class was in a brain.
She didn't know that everything was totally out of control.
And we couldn't tell her!

SOMETIMES YOUR BRAIN MAKES MISTAKES
by Wanda

FOOL YOUR BRAIN WITH THESE OPTICAL ILLUSIONS.

WHICH DRESS IS BIGGER?

Both are the same size!
But because of the background, your brain "thinks" the red dress is smaller.
Measure and see.

IS IT AN A OR AN H ?

READ THIS!

THE CAT

These two letters are shaped exactly the same. But because of the words they are in, your brain tells you one is an "H" and the other is an "A."

19

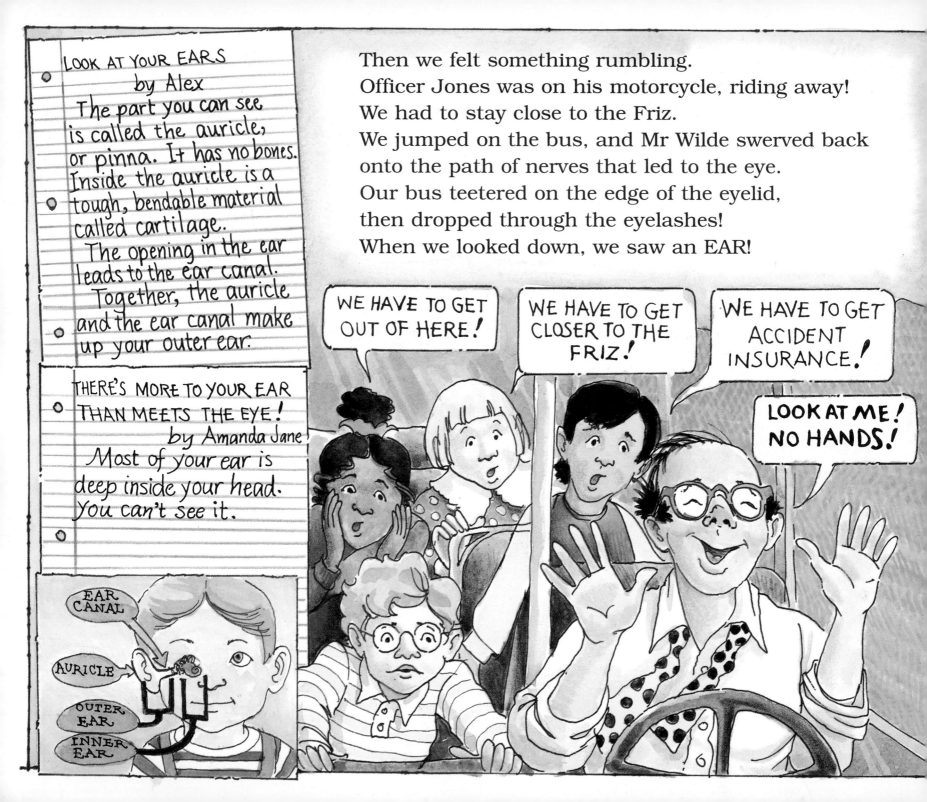

LOOK AT YOUR EARS
by Alex

The part you can see is called the auricle, or pinna. It has no bones. Inside the auricle is a tough, bendable material called cartilage.

The opening in the ear leads to the ear canal.

Together, the auricle and the ear canal make up your outer ear.

THERE'S MORE TO YOUR EAR THAN MEETS THE EYE!
by Amanda Jane

Most of your ear is deep inside your head. You can't see it.

EAR CANAL
AURICLE
OUTER EAR
INNER EAR

Then we felt something rumbling.
Officer Jones was on his motorcycle, riding away!
We had to stay close to the Friz.
We jumped on the bus, and Mr Wilde swerved back onto the path of nerves that led to the eye.
Our bus teetered on the edge of the eyelid, then dropped through the eyelashes!
When we looked down, we saw an EAR!

WE HAVE TO GET OUT OF HERE!

WE HAVE TO GET CLOSER TO THE FRIZ!

WE HAVE TO GET ACCIDENT INSURANCE!

LOOK AT ME! NO HANDS!

We were falling into the ear of a little kid who was looking in a toy store window. We went straight into his ear canal. *Whoosh!* We slid all the way down.

HERE WE COME!

I THINK YOU MEAN **EAR** WE COME!

TIME TO LEAVE, RICHIE.

COMING, MOM.

CAN YOU WIGGLE YOUR AURICLES?
by Carlos

Some people can move their outer ears. So can many animals. Animals that have large auricles use them as collectors to funnel sounds into the ear.

STORE HOURS
PLAYTIME
NAPTIME
BATHTIME
MEALTIME

WHAT ARE SOUND WAVES?
by Tim
When something moves back and forth rapidly, the air around it moves, too. These movements are sound waves, or vibrations.

WHEN A BELL RINGS
by Rachel

1. Clapper hits bell.
2. Bell vibrates.
3. Sound waves go through air.
4. Waves enter your ear.
5. Your hearing system starts to work.
6. You hear the bell ring!

At the end of the ear canal, we hit
a thin, stretchy membrane called the eardrum.
We came tumbling out of the bus
just as some sound waves entered the ear.
They made the eardrum vibrate.
We vibrated right along — through the eardrum
and into the middle ear. So did our bus.

EARDRUMS SURE ARE BOUNCY.

THAT MUST MAKE THEM VIBRATE BETTER.

JUST LIKE REAL DRUMS.

LET'S GO, RICHIE

FRIZZLE WARNING
Take care of your drums! Never put anything in your ear... especially not a busload of children!

There was nothing in the middle ear
except air and three ossicles —
small bones that carry sound vibrations.
Sound waves traveled from one bone to the next.
We went, too, and the bus rolled behind us.

Then we came to another stretchy membrane.
This one was called the oval window.
The last ossicle, the stirrup, was resting right on top of it.
Dorothy Ann read from Ms. Frizzle's notes, "Children, the oval window separates the middle ear from the inner ear."
"Inner ear, here we come!" shouted Wanda, as we went through.
We were going to the inner ear — whether we liked it or not!

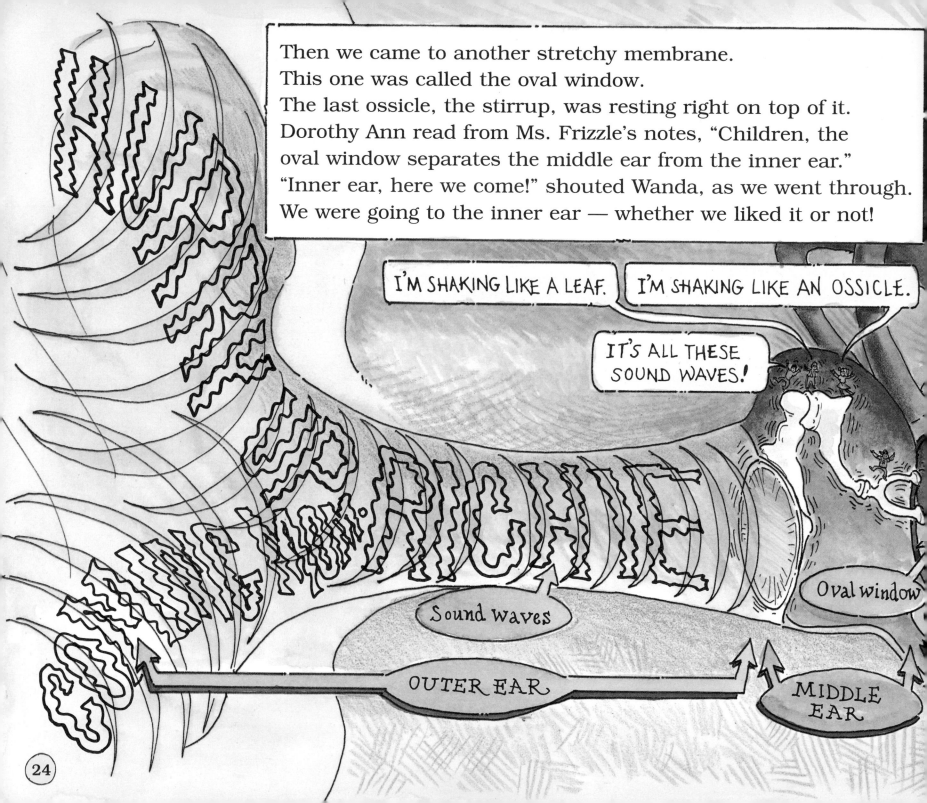

I'M SHAKING LIKE A LEAF.

I'M SHAKING LIKE AN OSSICLE.

IT'S ALL THESE SOUND WAVES!

Oval window

Sound waves

OUTER EAR

MIDDLE EAR

So far, all the parts of the ear had only one job —
to *carry* vibrations.
In the inner ear, we saw the part that
receives vibrations — the cochlea.
We swam through the liquid inside the cochlea.
We saw cells that looked like tiny hairs.
Ms. Frizzle's notes said, "Hair cells are sound receptors.
They translate sound vibrations into nerve signals."
As soon as we were on the bus again, Mr. Wilde
followed the nerve signals along the auditory nerve.

CAN YOU COMB YOUR HAIR CELLS?
by John
No! Hair cells aren't really hairs. They just look like them.

The hair cells in your ear have the same kind of job as the cones and rods in your eye.
Both kinds of cells take in a form of energy-- either light or sound waves-- and change it into nerve signals.

WOW! I GET TO DRIVE INTO THE BRAIN TWICE!

ONCE WAS NOT ENOUGH?

AUDITORY NERVE
(carries signals to the brain)

ANOTHER WORD FROM DOROTHY ANN
Cochlea comes from a word that means "snail."
The cochlea in your ear looks like a snail shell.

INNER EAR

FRIZZLE WARNING
Very loud noises can damage the hair cells in your inner ears.
THIS INCLUDES LOUD MUSIC!
TURN DOWN THE VOLUME!

COCHLEA
SNAIL
D.A. IN A SNAIL COSTUME

This time, we went to a different part of the cortex —
the hearing center for the ear we were in.
As soon as we were standing on it,
we could somehow hear what the little kid heard.
It was Ms. Frizzle reading from her "Things-to-Do" list.
She was nearby! Maybe there was still hope.
Maybe the Friz could rescue us!

"NUMBER THREE: HAVE PIZZA WITH M."

WHAT DOES "M" STAND FOR?

MAYBE SHE'S MEETING A FRIEND NAMED MARY OR MATTHEW...

MAYBE SHE WANTS MUSHROOMS ON HER PIZZA.

IT COULD MEAN ANYTHING.

NO, "ANYTHING" STARTS WITH "A."

WHERE ARE YOUR HEARING CENTERS? by Carmen
Put your two hands on your head just above your ears.
Your hands are right over the hearing centers on the cortex of your brain.

HEARING CENTER

VISION CENTER

FRIZZLE FACT
you can't hear with your ☉EARS☉ alone.
you need your 🧠 too!
BRAIN

footer: 26

Then we heard heels clicking on the sidewalk.
They were Ms. Frizzle's heels! She was walking away!
We had to follow her, so we ran for the bus.
We sped over the brain, into the auditory nerve,
through the ear, and out the ear canal.
Then we started falling!

This time there was no soft ear to catch us.
We saw the hard sidewalk rushing up at us!
Then, just before our bus crashed,
something amazing happened.
A friendly dog, smelling her way along Main Street,
snuffed us up.

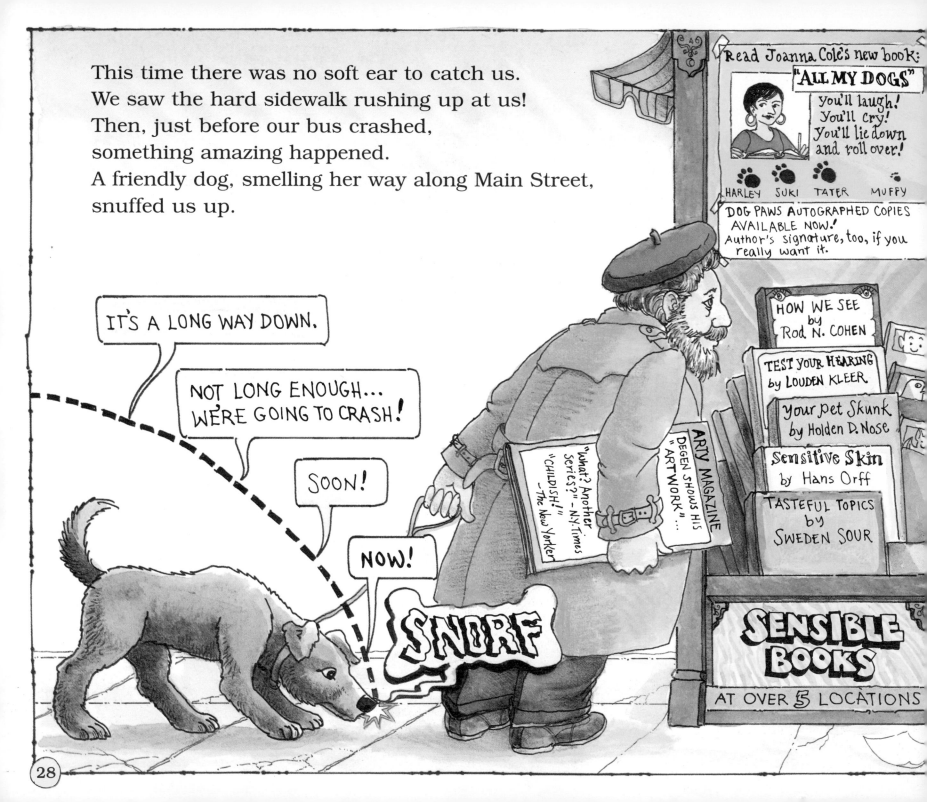

IT'S A LONG WAY DOWN.

NOT LONG ENOUGH... WE'RE GOING TO CRASH!

SOON!

NOW!

SNORF

HOW WE SEE by Rod N. COHEN

TEST YOUR HEARING by LOUDEN KLEER

Your Pet Skunk by Holden D. Nose

Sensitive Skin by Hans Orff

TASTEFUL TOPICS by SWEDEN SOUR

"What? Another Series?" – N.Y. Times
"CHILDISH!" – The New Yorker

ARTY MAGAZINE
DEGEN SHOWS HIS "ARTWORK"...

SENSIBLE BOOKS
AT OVER 5 LOCATIONS

28

At first we were happy because we were safe.
Then the full impact of our situation hit us.
We were inside a dog's nose!

THIS IS A NIGHTMARE!

IT'S SLIMY, TOO.

WE'LL NEVER FIND MS. FRIZZLE NOW!

WISDOM from the FRIZ-DOM

Never say never!

DOGS ARE SUPER SMELLERS
by Arnold
Dogs can smell odors that are very, very faint or very, very far away. Bloodhounds can tell one person from another just from the scent that comes through their shoes.

...AND IT'S TIME TO CHANGE YOUR SOCKS!

MY STUDENTS HAVE A NOSE FOR ADVENTURE.

NOT ME!

Mr. Wilde drove to one of the smell areas. Then we could smell what the dog smelled. It was easy to tell when we were close to the pizza restaurant!

SNIFF SNIFF!
Try this:
Smell something nice.
Now sniff.
Is the smell stronger?
That's because more odor went up to your smell patches.

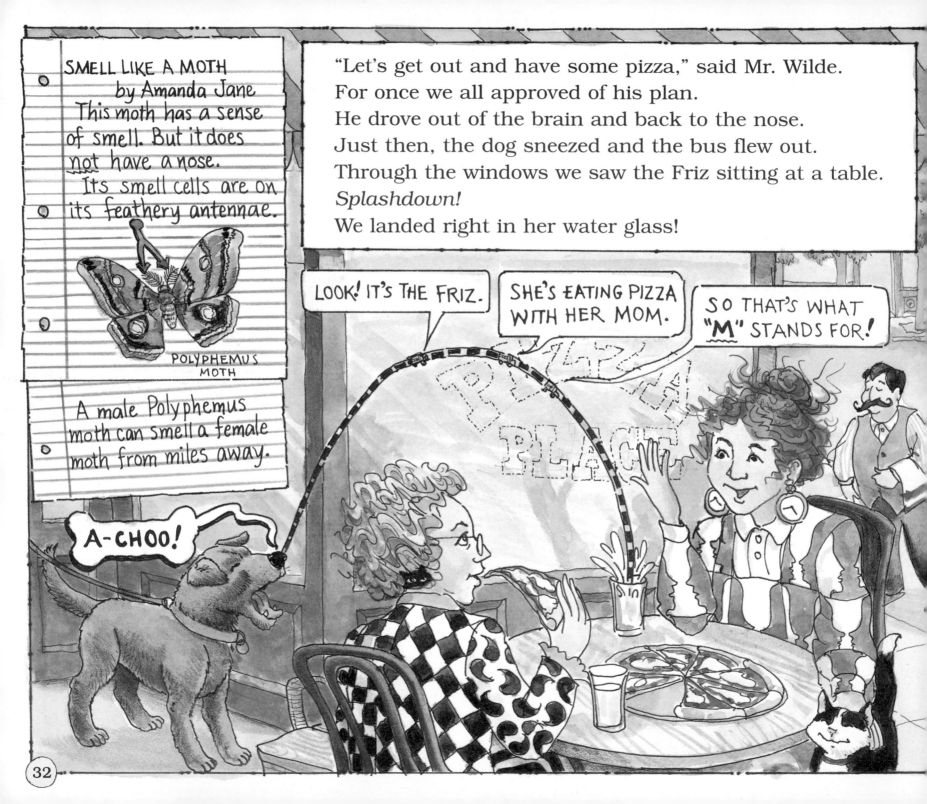

SMELL LIKE A MOTH
    by Amanda Jane
This moth has a sense of smell. But it does not have a nose.
    Its smell cells are on its feathery antennae.

POLYPHEMUS MOTH

A male Polyphemus moth can smell a female moth from miles away.

"Let's get out and have some pizza," said Mr. Wilde.
For once we all approved of his plan.
He drove out of the brain and back to the nose.
Just then, the dog sneezed and the bus flew out.
Through the windows we saw the Friz sitting at a table.
Splashdown!
We landed right in her water glass!

LOOK! IT'S THE FRIZ.

SHE'S EATING PIZZA WITH HER MOM.

SO THAT'S WHAT "M" STANDS FOR!

A-CHOO!

The bus got a good washing — it needed one!
Then a waiter accidently knocked over the glass.
We were tossed onto Ms. Frizzle's pizza!
Mr. Wilde tried to get away, but the pizza had extra cheese.
While we were spinning our wheels, the Friz decided to take a bite!

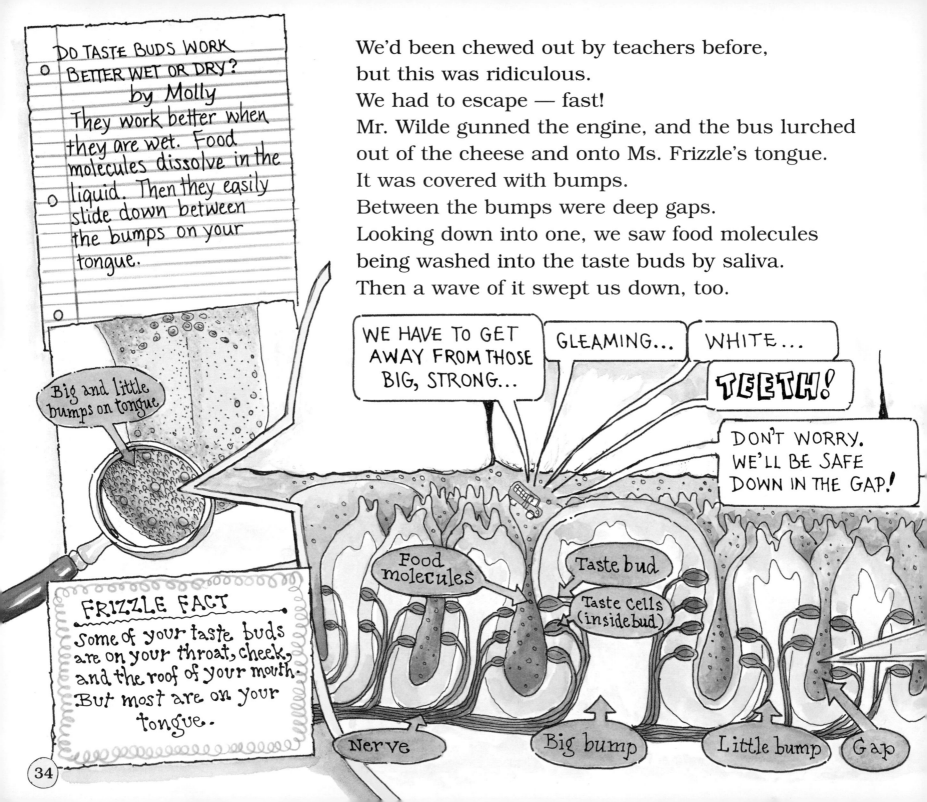

We'd been chewed out by teachers before,
but this was ridiculous.
We had to escape — fast!
Mr. Wilde gunned the engine, and the bus lurched
out of the cheese and onto Ms. Frizzle's tongue.
It was covered with bumps.
Between the bumps were deep gaps.
Looking down into one, we saw food molecules
being washed into the taste buds by saliva.
Then a wave of it swept us down, too.

We could have hidden out in the gap
until Ms. Frizzle finished chewing.
But that must have seemed too boring to Mr. Wilde.
He had school-bus fever.
He hung a sharp left into one of the taste buds.
The taste cells inside the bud
were changing the tastes into nerve messages.

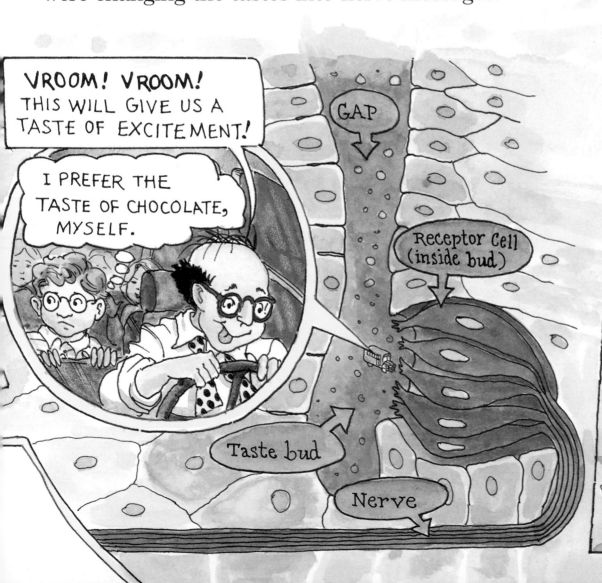

VROOM! VROOM!
THIS WILL GIVE US A
TASTE OF EXCITEMENT!

I PREFER THE
TASTE OF CHOCOLATE,
MYSELF.

GAP

Receptor Cell
(inside bud)

Taste bud

Nerve

YOUR SENSE OF SMELL
HELPS YOU TASTE
    by Gregory
When you chew, food
molecules go into the air
in your mouth.
    Then the air flows up
the back of your throat
and into your nose.
    When your nostrils are
closed, the air cannot flow.
That's why you may not
taste much when you
have a cold.

Smell
Cells

Tongue

Food

HERE ARE THE RECEPTOR
CELLS THE KIDS HAVE
VISITED SO FAR:

Rods and Cones
in the eye,

Hair Cells
in the ear,

Smell cells
in the nose,

and Taste cells
in the tongue.

HOW MANY FLAVORS CAN YOU TASTE?
by Ralphie

Our taste cells can detect <u>only four</u> tastes: bitter, sour, salty, and sweet.
   But people can taste over 10,000 different flavors. How is this possible?

IT'S CHOCOLATE!

Scientists say all the flavors we taste are mixtures of the four basic tastes, combined with the many different smells from foods.

FRIZZLE FACT
You can't taste with your mouth alone.
You need your brain, too.

36

Before we knew it, we were traveling on a pathway of nerves to a taste area of Ms. Frizzle's brain. We climbed off the bus and stood on her taste cortex. Now we could taste what our teacher tasted!

WAHOO! IT'S OUR <u>FOURTH</u> VISIT TO A BRAIN.

THIS TIME IT'S MS. FRIZZLE'S BRAIN!!!

UH-OH! THIS COULD BE OUR MOST DANGEROUS TRIP YET!

TASTE CENTER

ANCHOVY

PIZZA

TONGUE

FRIZZLY HAIR

TASTE NERVE

We thought we'd love the taste of Ms. Frizzle's pizza.
But — yuck! — it was covered with *ANCHOVIES!*
We were so grossed out that we ran away
from the taste area of the brain as fast as we could!
Luckily, Mr. Wilde followed us in the bus.

BLAAA-AAH!
THIS PIZZA IS AWFUL!

HASN'T SHE HEARD
OF PEPPERONI?

DON'T TALK—
RUN!

WAIT FOR ME!

Taste sensations

CATFISH WIN THE TASTE
CONTEST
by Wanda
A catfish may have the
most taste buds of any
animal. It has 175,000.
That's about 50 times
as many as the average
human.
Most of the taste buds
are on the <u>outside</u> of
the catfish's body.
It can taste the food
before eating it.

I CAN TASTE
WITH MY BACK
AND MY SIDES
AND MY HEAD.

CHICKENS COME IN LAST
by John
Chickens can taste, but
not very well. They
have only <u>24</u>
taste buds.

TWENTY-FOUR
IS PLENTY FOR
ME, THANKS.

AFTER ALL,
IT'S ONLY
CHICKEN FEED.

YOUR SKIN IS A
SENSE ORGAN
by Carmen

Receptor cells in your skin send nerve messages to the "touch" center of your brain.

Your skin senses include not only touch, but also temperature, itch, pressure, and pain.

THE TOUCH AREA OF
THE CORTEX
by Tim

Each part of your body has its own special section on the touch area of the brain.

We ended up on the part of the brain that gets touch messages from the hand. Once we were standing on it, we could somehow feel what Ms. Frizzle felt! When she felt something hot or cold, or hard or soft, we did too!

"Let's see where this nerve goes," said Mr. Wilde.
Back on the bus, we zoomed along the nerve pathways leading away from Ms. Frizzle's brain.
At the end of the nerves were the receptor cells in her skin.

WE'RE TRAVELING TO MS. FRIZZLE'S SKIN.

IT TAKES A LOT OF NERVE TO GO THERE.

WHISKERS ARE
TOUCH ORGANS
by Shirley
Cats, dogs, mice, horses, and many other mammals have sensitive whiskers. Whiskers help animals find their way in the dark. A whisker may also detect food that the animal does not see.

WHOA! I ALMOST MISSED THAT ONE!

LOOK AT ALL THE WEIRD RECEPTOR CELLS IN HERE.

Pore

Receptor for vibration

NOTE: These whiskers are not sense organs.

Receptor for heat, itching, and pain

Receptor for change in shape and extreme cold

ENLARGEMENT OF A SECTION OF SKIN

Receptor for light touch

Sweat gland

Hair follicle receptor

Receptor for deep pressure

39

Q: WHERE IS YOUR SENSE OF BALANCE?
A: IN YOUR EARS!
by Phoebe

In the inner ear, there are three hollow tubes called the semicircular canals.
Hair cells in the canals send messages to your brain about your body's movement.
Then your brain tells your muscles to adjust so your body won't fall.

"Here's our exit," said Mr. Wilde, driving out through a pore in the skin. Up ahead, we saw the Friz petting her mom's nice soft cat. Mr. Wilde drove so fast that the bus flew right off Ms. Frizzle's hand and into the cat's inner ear.

NOT ANOTHER EAR!

WHAT A CATASTROPHE!

FRED

THE HUMAN EAR

Semicircular Canals are for balance.

Hair cells

Nerve

Cochlea is for hearing.

MIDDLE EAR

INNER EAR

EARS AREN'T JUST FOR HEARING.

THEY KEEP YOU UPRIGHT, TOO!

RATATAT RATAT

We passed the snail-shaped cochlea used for hearing.
Then we came to some hollow tubes.
They are used for balancing.
We hung on for dear life as we felt the cat jump.
Next, we heard the rumble of a car engine.
"Seat belts, everyone," yelled Ms. Frizzle, and off we went.

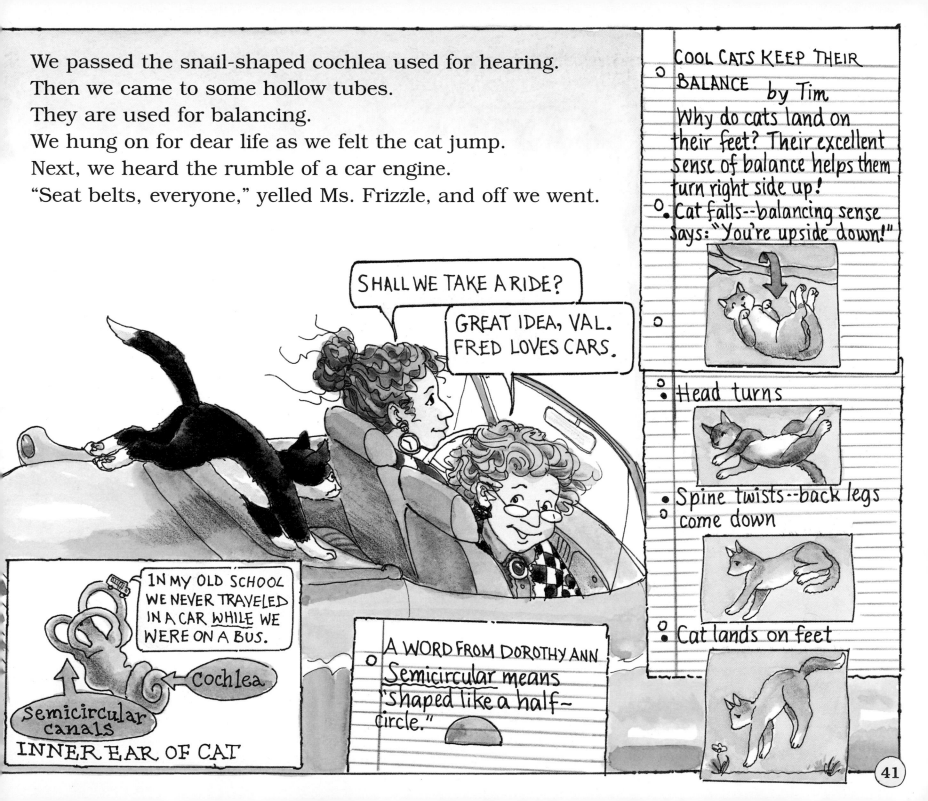

SHALL WE TAKE A RIDE?

GREAT IDEA, VAL. FRED LOVES CARS.

IN MY OLD SCHOOL WE NEVER TRAVELED IN A CAR WHILE WE WERE ON A BUS.

← Cochlea

Semicircular canals

INNER EAR OF CAT

A WORD FROM DOROTHY ANN
Semicircular means "shaped like a half-circle."

COOL CATS KEEP THEIR BALANCE   by Tim

Why do cats land on their feet? Their excellent sense of balance helps them turn right side up!

Cat falls--balancing sense says: "You're upside down!"

Head turns

Spine twists--back legs come down

Cat lands on feet

41

When the Friz made a sudden swerve,
we were *cata*pulted out of the ear.
We landed in the road behind Ms. Frizzle's car.
As the bus grew to its regular size again,
Mr. Wilde beeped the horn, and Ms. Frizzle pulled over.

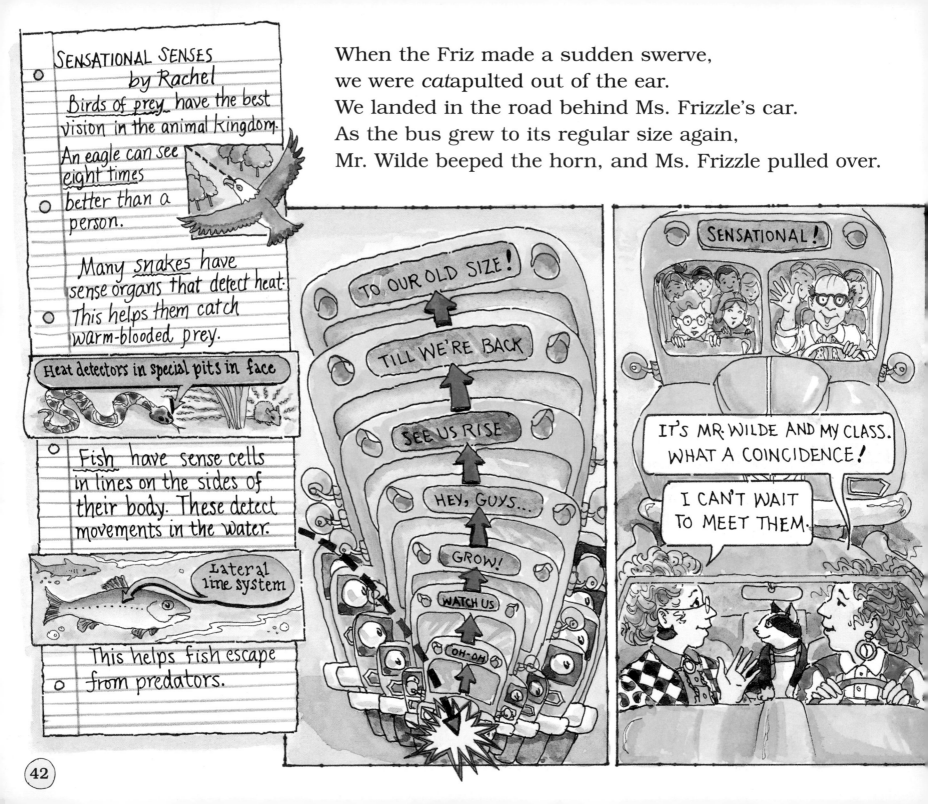

SENSATIONAL SENSES
by Rachel

<u>Birds of prey</u> have the best vision in the animal kingdom. An eagle can see eight times better than a person.

Many <u>snakes</u> have sense organs that detect heat. This helps them catch warm-blooded prey.

Heat detectors in special pits in face

<u>Fish</u> have sense cells in lines on the sides of their body. These detect movements in the water.

Lateral line system

This helps fish escape from predators.

TO OUR OLD SIZE!
TILL WE'RE BACK
SEE US RISE
HEY, GUYS...
GROW!
WATCH US
OH-OH

SENSATIONAL!

IT'S MR. WILDE AND MY CLASS. WHAT A COINCIDENCE!

I CAN'T WAIT TO MEET THEM.

We told her about the meeting, and in no time we were all on our way back to school.

ONLY FIVE?
YOU'VE GOT TO BE KIDDING!
by Michael

Everyone says there are FIVE SENSES because long ago we knew about only five: seeing, hearing, smelling, tasting, and touching.

Today scientists have found about TWENTY senses in humans and animals combined.

For example, there are senses that detect gravity, electricity, ultraviolet light, and more!

We got there just in time to sing our song
and check out the refreshment table.
Then — what a surprise — Ms. Frizzle got an award.
If anyone deserves an award, it's the Friz.
She's the most *sense*-ational teacher in school!